W9-AAQ-295

THOMAS FORD MEMORIAL LIBRARY
WESTERN SPRINGS, ILLINOIS

JUL 99

GAYLORD M

A Mouse
Called Wolf

ALSO BY DICK KING-SMITH

Babe: The Gallant Pig
Harry's Mad
Martin's Mice
Ace: The Very Important Pig
The Toby Man
Paddy's Pot of Gold
Pretty Polly
The Invisible Dog
Three Terrible Trins
Harriet's Hare
The Stray

DICK KING-SMITH

A Mouse
Called Wolf

ILLUSTRATED BY JON GOODELL

THOMAS FORD MEMORIAL LIBRARY
WESTERN SPRINGS, IL 60558

CROWN PUBLISHERS, INC., NEW YORK

Text copyright © 1997 by Fox Busters, Ltd.
Illustrations copyright © 1997 by Jon Goodell.

All rights reserved. No part of this book may be reproduced or
transmitted in any form or by any means, electronic or mechanical,
including photocopying, recording, or by any information storage
and retrieval system, without permission in writing
from the publisher.

Published by Crown Publishers, Inc., a Random House company,
201 East 50th Street, New York, New York 10022. Published in
Great Britain by Transworld in 1997.

CROWN is a trademark of Crown Publishers, Inc.

http://www.randomhouse.com/

Printed in the United States of America

Library of Congress Cataloging-in-Publication Data
King-Smith, Dick.
A mouse called Wolf / Dick King-Smith ; illustrated by Jon Goodell.
p.   cm.
ISBN 0-517-70973-2 (trade)
ISBN 0-517-70974-0 (lib. bdg.)
Summary: A mouse with an unusual name shares his
musical gift with a widowed concert pianist.
[1. Mice—Fiction. 2. Music—Fiction.] I. Goodell, Jon, ill. II. Title.
PZ7.K5893Mon   1997
[Fic]—dc21   97-1526

10 9 8 7 6 5 4 3 2 1

First American Edition

- CONTENTS -

1	A Name	1
2	A Joke	7
3	A Song	14
4	A Trap	22
5	A Lesson	31
6	A Lure	39
7	A Reward	49
8	A Groan	58
9	A Rescue	68
10	A Composer	79
11	A Recital	86

ONE

A Name

WOLFGANG AMADEUS MOUSE was the youngest of thirteen children. He was also the smallest. His mother had given the other twelve mouse pups quite ordinary names, like Bill or Jane.

But when she looked at her last-born and saw that he was only half as big as his brothers and sisters, she said to herself, "He should have an important-sounding name to make up for his lack of size. On second

thought, he should have two important-sounding names. But what
should they be?"

Now, it so happened that this
particular mother mouse lived in a
house belonging to a lady who
played the piano. It was a grand
piano that stood close to a living
room wall, so that its left front leg
almost touched the molding. In the
molding, hidden from the human eye
by the piano leg, was a hole. In this
hole lived the mother mouse (whose
name was Mary).

One night, when the lady of the
house had played a final tune on the
piano and gone to bed, Mary came
out of the hole in the molding. She
ran up the left front leg and onto the
keyboard, which as usual had been

left open, and bounced along over the keys. But even though she was heavy with young, she was still much too light to make any noise.

Then she saw that a single sheet of music had been left lying on the piano stool.

"Just what I need to start making my nest with," said Mary Mouse, and by pushing at the sheet (a piece of piano music by Mozart) with her little forepaws, she managed to send it sailing down to the floor. Because it was too big to drag through the mousehole, she cut it up into smaller pieces with her sharp teeth and pulled the pieces inside.

Over the next day Mary chewed these small pieces of paper into shreds, and with them built herself a

most comfortable nest. In this, in due course, she gave birth to her thirteen pups. Only when they were several days old, and she had made the decision that the thirteenth and littlest must have not one but two names, and important-sounding names at that, did something catch her eye.

It was a scrap of the sheet music that had somehow escaped being chewed up, and it had some writing on it.

Mary got out of her nest to inspect it. It said:

WOLFGANG AMADEUS MO

Mary gave a squeak of delight. "Perfect!" she cried to all the blind and naked pups. Then she softly whispered in the littlest one's ear, "This name was specially designed for you, dear. I feel it in my bones. Why, to be sure, the last three letters of the third word are missing, but there's no doubt what they were. The smallest you may be, but these names will make you the greatest, Wolfgang Amadeus Mouse!"

TWO

A Joke

A FEW WEEKS later the mouse pups began to venture out of the hole in the molding at night. Before long they learned to climb up the left front leg of the grand piano, and they played on the keyboard.

In particular they liked to race along the keys. Sometimes they were flat races along the fifty-two white keys from bass to treble, and sometimes they were hurdle races over the thirty-six raised black keys. Some nights one pup would win, some nights another, but Wolfgang Amadeus, being so small, was always last. He found the hurdles difficult to get over, and quite often in the flat races the rush of his bigger brothers and sisters running past him would cause him to lose his footing on the slippery white keys and fall to the floor.

Luckily the room was thickly carpeted, and he would fall very lightly, usually landing on his feet without harm. But the others of course just laughed as they peered over the edge and looked down on him.

They were not very nice to him, partly on account of his lack of size, partly because it seemed to them that he was his mother's favorite, but

mostly on account of his long name. All the time they heard Mary Mouse's anxious voice crying, "Wolfgang Amadeus! Wolfgang Amadeus! Where are you? Are you all right? Did you hurt yourself falling off the piano, Wolfgang Amadeus?"

At first Bill and Jane and Tom and Ann and all the rest teased their little brother—out of their mother's earshot—about his strange long name, and they even made up a rhyme that they squeaked at him all together (especially every time he fell off the piano).

"Who is small and meek and mild?
Who is Mommy's favorite child?
Who's no bigger than a louse?
Wolfgang Amadeus Mouse!"

All this made Wolfgang Amadeus unhappy, and one day he said to his mother, "Mommy, why do I have to have such a long name when all the others have short ones?"

"Because yours is an important-sounding one, Wolfgang Amadeus," replied Mary, "and you are going to grow up to be an important mouse. You cannot have a short name."

But in the end he did, given to him by the other pups.

They had been playing another one of their favorite games, which took place on top of the grand piano. They would line up on the curved edge at the back of the instrument, and then each one in turn would see how far he or she could slide across its highly polished gleaming surface.

One after another they would run and then slide on their fat furry little tummies. The object was to reach the straight front edge of the piano top without falling over and down onto the keyboard below. Sometimes they did fall over, but it was only a short drop and they would soon scramble back up again, squeaking with laughter.

One night when they were playing this sliding game, one of them called out to another, "Look at that Wolfgang Amadeus! He's hopeless! He never gets more than halfway across. He can't get up enough speed. His legs aren't long enough!"

"There's only one thing long about him," said the other, "and that's his name. I can't get my tongue around it. It's too much of a mouseful."

"Well, okay. Let's shorten it."

"What shall we call him, then?"

"Just Wolf."

"Wolf?" cried the other voices. "What a joke! Tee-hee-hee! A mouse called Wolf!" And they all giggled at their little brother, not caring, as usual, whether his feelings were hurt.

They could not know that in fact he was delighted.

THREE

A Song

WOLF WAS EVEN more delighted when his twelve brothers and sisters left home.

For some time Mary Mouse's milk supply had been dwindling, and the pups had become used to accompanying their mother on her nightly scrounge. Around the house they would go in the wee hours of the night, especially to the kitchen and the dining room. They traveled by a system of mouseways, searching the floors and tables and cupboards for anything edible.

Soon the bolder ones stopped coming back to the hole by the piano leg, and before long it was only Wolf who returned home. He felt safer with his mother, and she was pleased to have him still at home with her. He in turn was pleased that she had become used to hearing the others use his shortened name, and now did so too, only addressing him as "Wolfgang Amadeus" if she was angry with him (which was seldom).

All through the first weeks of his life Wolf had been used to hearing the sound of the piano, for the lady of the house played every day.

The other pups grumbled at the music.

"What a racket!" they muttered to one another. "How are we expected to get a good day's sleep?"

But Wolf grew to like the noise very much, and now, alone (Mary slept through it), he began to listen carefully to the melodies.

The lady usually played her piano twice each day—in the late morning and then again in the early evening. The evening recital was the one Wolf enjoyed most, because by then he was rested and awake. He began sitting in the mouth of the hole by the piano leg and listening to the music above his head.

He found that even when the playing stopped, he could still hear a particular tune inside his head, and he would hum it to himself—in a kind of silent hum—as he followed his mother about on the night's foraging.

"I wish mice could sing," he said to his mother, "instead of just squeaking. I'd love to be able to sing."

Mary had not had a very successful scavenge and was tired and hungry.

"Mice...*sing?*" she cried. "Don't be such a stupid child, Wolfgang Amadeus."

Now she's annoyed at me, thought Wolf, and he said no more on the subject. But he couldn't stop thinking about it. The next day, in fact, he actually dreamed that he was singing.

When he awoke, it was early afternoon, a time, had he known it, when the lady of the house always had a little nap after her lunch. Mary

Mouse was also fast asleep, so Wolf crept quietly out of the mousehole, scaled the piano leg, walked along the keyboard, and sat down on middle C, just below the elegant lettering that said:

STEINWAY & SONS

He sat there thinking of a particular tune. It was a favorite of the lady's and she often played it, so he knew it by heart.

If only mice could sing, thought Wolf. Now is the perfect moment, here is the perfect place, and this is the perfect song for me. He sighed.

"Ah, me!" he said. "Perhaps, though I can't sing it, I could try to squeak it." And he threw back his head and opened his mouth.

Then, to his total surprise, out of that little mouth came a high clear lovely little voice that sang every note of the melody to perfection. Wolf was singing like a bird, except no songbird in the world could have sung as beautifully.

"La-la-la!" he caroled, for of course he knew no words to the music. But it did not matter, for by chance the piece he had chosen was from a book of folk tunes by Mendelssohn called *Songs Without Words*.

Long and loudly sang Wolf, repeating the melody again and again in the ecstasy of discovery that to say mice could not sing was not entirely true. One mouse could! But before he finally fell silent, others in the house were awakened by his long, loud solo.

Mary came out of a deep sleep and her hole and climbed the piano leg. Her mouth fell open in utter amazement, but no sound came from it.

In various holes in various rooms Wolf's brothers and sisters grumbled at this strange noise that had awakened them.

Snoozing on her bed, the lady of the house thought she heard, some-

where downstairs, a familiar tune by Mendelssohn, decided she'd been dreaming, and went back to sleep.

But there was one pair of ears in the kitchen that caught the sound of Wolf's singing and aroused in their owner a certain curiosity. The cat jumped out of its bed beside the stove and stretched, spreading its claws wide before padding silently toward the living room.

- FOUR -

A Trap

"BEAUTIFUL, WOLF. THAT was quite beautiful!" cried Mary as the song came to an end. "Oh! To think that I am the mother of the world's first singing mouse!" And she ran along the keyboard to nuzzle her child affectionately.

"You're a genius!" she said. "Sing me something else, like a good boy."

"What would you like, Mommy?" asked Wolf, but his mother did not answer.

Instead she suddenly crouched on the keys, still as a stone, her hair on end, her eyes bulging in obvious terror as she stared over the singer's shoulder.

Looking quickly behind him, Wolf saw the cat creeping across the carpet, head raised, yellow eyes staring up at the two mice on the piano. It gathered itself to spring.

Wolf saw immediately that jumping down to the floor would be suicide. The cat would catch one or both of them before they had time to reach the safety of their hole.

"Quick, Mommy!" he cried. "Follow me!" And with a mighty effort he scrabbled his way up over STEIN-WAY & SONS and into the body of the grand piano, Mary hard on his heels.

It is doubtful that the mice might somehow have been able to escape the cat in the network of taut wires that formed the piano strings, but Fate now took a hand in the proceedings.

The cat's leap took it up onto the right-hand edge of the piano, but its landing was an unfortunate one, for the cat hit the prop stick (which held the top of the instrument open) and dislodged it. Supported no longer, the heavy top began to fall, and instantly, with that lightning reaction cats have, the attacker wheeled to jump back down again.

But the cat was not quite quick enough.

The top of the piano fell shut, not with quite the loud crash you would

have expected, but with a slightly more muffled noise. Caught between the top and the body of the piano was an inch of ginger tail. Then the force of the fall of the piano top made it bounce just a fraction. The cat fell free and rushed from the living room at full speed.

In the days that followed, the squashed and bruised tip of the cat's tail healed, but in its mind the cat carried the scars of that encounter for the rest of its life.

Far from realizing that what had happened was its own fault, the cat felt sure, then and forever, that it was the mice who had engineered the whole thing.

It was the mice who woke me up with their noise, the cat thought, who lured me into the room, who jumped inside the piano knowing that I would follow. It was the mice who somehow sprang that trap that caught my tail in its jaws.

Little did Mary and Wolf realize, but from that moment on the cat would never again pose a threat to them. From then on, unknown to them, they were to live in a house with a cat that was forevermore scared stiff of mice.

Now all they knew was that they were prisoners.

Fearfully they explored the blackness of the inside of the closed piano, looking for some way out but finding none. All the time, as they crisscrossed the tightly stretched strings, their feet made a discordant jingle of tiny sounds, a little tinkling sonata for two mice and piano.

At last, tired out by the difficulty of keeping their balance on all those dozens of tightropes, they crouched side by side in the darkness.

"Oh, Wolfgang Amadeus!" Mary sighed.

"Not angry with me, are you, Mommy?" asked Wolf.

"No, dear, no. I only used your full name because I was thinking how splendid it would have sounded if you had become a famous singer. Which now you never will."

"Why not, Mommy?" asked Wolf.

"Because we are fated to die here on this cold bed of wires, you and I."

"No, we aren't, Mommy," said Wolf. "The lady plays the piano every evening, and always with the top up. She'll come along soon and raise it, and then we can make a run for home."

"Home," said Mary heavily. "Something tells me I will never see it again. If the lady does lift the lid, which I doubt, it'll only be to put the cat in."

"Cheer up, Mommy," said Wolf. "I'll sing you a song."

He thought of a tune that the lady occasionally played in the evenings as the light outside faded and the living room grew gradually darker in the gathering dusk, and he sat up on his haunches and began to sing this song. Its name or the words to it he did not know, of course, and could not have understood, but its gentle melody seemed to him about right for calming an overanxious mother.

So intent was Wolf on his singing and so lost in admiration was the listening Mary that neither heard footsteps approaching the grand piano.

Very slowly, very quietly, the lady of the house opened the top of her instrument to see within a mouse watching another, smaller mouse. The smaller mouse was, to her complete shock, singing an old ballad in a high, pure, true voice. There was not the shadow of a doubt about the tune. It was "Love's Old Sweet Song."

- FIVE -

A Lesson

WOLF HAD HIS back turned as the piano lid was slowly opened. What's more, in the sheer pleasure of exercising his newfound talent, his eyes were shut tight as he caroled.

When the song ended, he opened them to see once again his mother staring over his shoulder in terror. Looking quickly behind him, he saw the huge round human face peering in, and once again he cried, "Quick, Mommy! Follow me!"

Out of the body of the piano they leaped, down onto the keyboard, turned a sharp right, whizzed along to the lowest of the bass keys, down the leg, and into their hole.

Carefully the lady replaced the prop stick and sat down on the piano stool. She did not notice the few ginger hairs stuck under the rim of the top. For a moment she wondered if this was some sort of dream, but she pinched herself hard and it hurt, so it wasn't.

"Oh!" she said quietly. "To think that in my house there lives the world's first singing mouse!"

She flexed her fingers to get the stiffness out of them and then began to play, very softly, "Love's Old Sweet Song."

Wouldn't it be lovely, she thought,

if that mouse came out again and sang to my accompaniment. But of course no such thing happened.

Mrs. Honeybee (for that was the lady's name) rose from the piano stool, got down on her hands and knees—with difficulty, for she was not young and her joints were creaky—and found the hole in the molding behind the left front leg of the piano.

Most people, on finding mice in their home, would think right away of traps and poison, or—if they had a cat—would hope that the cat would solve the problem. But no such thoughts entered Mrs. Honeybee's head. She loved all animals and could not bear the idea of killing anything, even a wasp or a fly.

The one thing that immediately worried her was the cat, which was a stray that had walked in one day and adopted Mrs. Honeybee. But now, finding that she had mice in the house, she realized what a threat the cat posed to them.

The cat might kill my singing mouse, she thought. It must never come in here again. She got to her feet and shut the door, not realizing that nothing could ever persuade her ginger cat to enter the living room again.

Seated once more at her piano, Mrs. Honeybee pondered what to play. In her youth she had been a concert pianist, and though rheumatism meant that her gifts were now limited, she still loved to play short pieces by her favorite classical composers—Brahms, Beethoven, and of course Mozart. She liked to play traditional songs and ballads and folk tunes as well.

It suddenly occurred to her to test out her singing mouse. It could have learned "Love's Old Sweet Song" only by sitting in that hole in the molding and listening to me playing it many times, she thought.

"All right, then, my mouse," said

Mrs. Honeybee. "I'll teach you another tune, something very simple, and we'll see how soon you can pick it up. What shall it be?"

And then, because she was thinking about the little animals, she said, "I know! 'Three Blind Mice'! It doesn't matter that there are only two of you with perfectly good eyesight. You couldn't understand the words anyway. All we need is the tune."

So for perhaps ten minutes old Mrs. Honeybee played "Three Blind Mice," again and again and again.

At first she just played the melody, but then she began to sing the words to the old nursery rhyme. A horrible woman, that farmer's wife, she thought as she sang.

Imagine cutting the tails off mice—and blind ones at that! How I hate cruelty to animals.

"There," she said, bending down toward the mousehole as the last notes died away, "you ought to have learned it by now." And she got up and left the living room, being careful to close the door.

Later that evening, after Mrs. Honeybee had fed herself and her cat and was on her way to bed, she couldn't resist going to listen outside the living room door, just in case the mouse might be singing. She put her ear to the keyhole, but all was silent within.

Mrs. Honeybee sighed, but before the sigh had even finished, she heard that high, pure, true voice begin to sing "Three Blind Mice."

But this time Wolf wasn't just singing "La-la-la." While practicing the new song in his head as Mrs. Honeybee was eating her dinner, he had made up some words for it.

Mrs. Honeybee couldn't know, of course, but this was what the mouse called Wolf was actually singing:

"Singsong mouse.
Singsong mouse.
Hark to his song.
Hark to his song.
He sings as sweetly as any bird
That anyone else in the world
    has heard.
Did you ever hear of a thing
    as absurd
As a singsong mouse?"

SIX

A Lure

THOUGH THEY COULD not have known it, Mrs. Honeybee and Mary Mouse had something in common. Both were widows.

Mr. Honeybee had died peacefully of heart failure many years ago, and the heart of Mary's mate had failed, not at all peacefully, after an unfortunate encounter with the cat.

But in another way Mrs. Honeybee and Mary were not at all alike.

Mary didn't miss her husband in the least. Mrs. Honeybee missed hers very much. Mary had her favorite young child at home with her. Mrs. Honeybee's children were middle-aged and lived far away, so she seldom saw them or her grandchildren.

In short, Mary was not lonely, but Mrs. Honeybee was.

For a while the ginger cat had given her someone to talk to, but now the animal seemed to have become a nervous wreck. The kitchen door needed oiling, and each time Mrs. Honeybee opened it, it gave out a mouselike squeak, whereupon the cat would leap from its basket and dash out through the cat flap.

Perhaps because of the piano player's loneliness, many of the tunes that Wolf listened to were rather sad-sounding ones. But one morning he was awakened by the sound of a rather lively tune. What's more, the lady was singing as she played.

In fact, Mrs. Honeybee, who talked to herself a lot, had given herself a good talking-to.

"Jane Honeybee," she said severely, "you are becoming a miserable old woman, and it shows in your choice of music. The next thing you know, you'll be playing the funeral march. You should count your blessings, my girl. How many other people do you suppose are lucky enough to have a singing mouse in their house? Why, none. So why don't you choose a happy piece of music to teach your mouse? Then it can sing it to you and cheer you up."

She thought for a while, and then

she smiled and began to play and sing a song that she remembered singing as a small girl:

> "Come on, everyone!
> Sing and dance and run!
> Making friends and
> Having a lot of fun!
>
> Even if it's raining
> And the skies are gray,
> Nobody's complaining—
> It's a lovely day.
>
> Come on, everyone!
> Sing and dance and run!
> Making friends and
> Having a lot of fun!"

"There!" said Mrs. Honeybee when she had played and sung the song several times. "You should have gotten it in your head by now, mouse. The tune, I mean, not the words." And she stood up, smiling to herself at the ridiculous idea of a mouse putting words to a song.

But that is exactly what Wolf now spent a long time doing.

"That was a happy tune, wasn't it, Mommy?" he said once the lady had left the room.

"She doesn't sing half as well as you do, dear," said Mary. "And, of course, I couldn't understand the words."

"I'll make some up for you," said Wolf.

That evening as Mrs. Honeybee sat down at her piano, she heard that voice again, somewhat muffled since it was coming from the depths of the mousehole. Though of course she could not understand the words Wolf had composed and was now trying out on his mother. And they were:

"Merry mice are we!
Mommy Mouse and me!
Hear me sing this
Lovely old melody!

You may chance to see us,
Lady of the house.
Wolfgang Amadeus
And Mom, who's Mary Mouse.

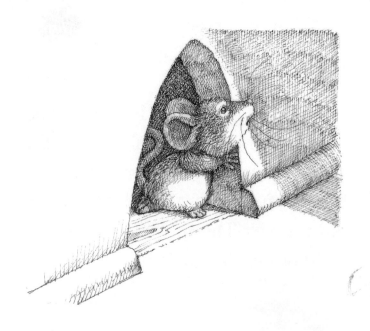

Merry mice are we!
Mommy Mouse and me!
Hear me sing this
Lovely old melody!"

When Wolf finished singing, he was startled by a sudden sharp noise. Peering cautiously out of the hole, he saw that the lady was sitting on the piano stool, clapping her hands together loudly.

"Bravo, mouse!" said Mrs. Honeybee. "You sing twice as well as I do. If only you would come out of your hole and climb up here on the piano, then I could accompany you as you sing."

"Silly old woman!" she went on to herself. "Accompanying a singing mouse! What a crazy idea. But then the idea of a mouse singing is crazy anyway, yet this one does, beautifully. One thing's obvious. I must make friends with him. Or her. Him, I somehow think, and I have a feeling the other, bigger one may be his mother. Now, what's the best way to make a friend of a mouse? Why, food, of course! But what sort?"

Then Mrs. Honeybee remembered hearing somewhere that mice

are especially fond of chocolate (as indeed she herself was). She got up and went across the living room to a small table. On it stood a tin in which she kept sweets. From the tin she took out a packet of chocolates. From the packet she took out one chocolate and then put the rest back in the tin and closed the lid.

She went over to the grand piano and, to avoid bending, carefully dropped the one chocolate beside the wheel on the piano's left front leg, outside the mousehole. Then she left the room, shutting the door behind her.

Before she went to bed, Mrs. Honeybee just couldn't resist going back to the living room.

"They probably haven't eaten it yet, I don't suppose," she said.

She turned on the light to see if the chocolate was still there. It wasn't.

"Good boy!" she said softly. "There's plenty more where that came from, if only you'll come out and sing for me."

SEVEN

A Reward

"THE BEST LAID schemes o' mice and men," said the poet Robert Burns, don't always turn out quite right. But maybe it's different with women.

At any rate, Mrs. Honeybee's plan for making friends with her singing mouse seemed likely, as the days went by, to be a winner.

The very next day after she had put down that first chocolate, she put another down in the same place just as she was about to begin her morning piano playing. No sooner had she played the first few bars of a tune (it was "Food, Glorious Food," from the musical *Oliver!*) than she saw from the corner of her eye a little mouse dart out of the hole in the molding, grab the chocolate, and whisk back in again.

"Look, Mommy," said Wolf as he laid the prize before his mother. "Another one of those yummy sweets!"

Mary, newly awakened, listened to the music above.

"Wolfgang Amadeus!" she said. "D'you mean to tell me you just went out and took it while the lady was actually playing?"

"Don't be angry, Mommy," said Wolf. "She's nice, I'm sure of it. She must feel kindly toward us, or she wouldn't be feeding us this stuff."

"It could be a trick," said Mary, but all the same she bit a lump out of the chocolate.

Mrs. Honeybee wisely did not hurry. Patience, she knew, was what was needed, and she took one step at a time.

After evening playing that day, she put out another chocolate, but not on the floor this time. Instead she placed it at the bass end of the key-board beside the bottom A.

"You'll have to climb for this one, mouse," she said.

By bedtime it was gone.

The following morning she put another in the same place, sat down, and began to play a song called

"Climb Ev'ry Mountain." Halfway through the song, she was delighted to see a mouse climbing up the piano leg. It sat beside the chocolate, watching her with bright eyes. Mrs. Honeybee continued playing, but in a higher key so that her left hand would not come too close to the mouse. After a few seconds, he took the candy in his mouth and ran down the leg of the piano and into the hole.

So it went on. Day by day Mrs. Honeybee lured the singing mouse upward and inward. She now played with the top of the piano closed, and once the mouse had grown accustomed to taking a chocolate at keyboard height, she began to place each fresh one up on the top, first at the left-hand edge and then gradually closer to the center of the instrument. Until at last the candy was directly above middle C, directly over STEIN-WAY & SONS, in fact, directly opposite the face of the pianist.

Although Wolf was by now quite used to collecting his prize from wherever it had been placed, confident that the lady would not harm him, he nevertheless did not usually stick around. But when at last he found himself sitting so close to her, their eyes on the same level and no more than a foot and a half apart, he paused for a moment before picking up the candy, and they looked directly at each other.

"Well done, mouse!" said Mrs. Honeybee quietly, and she began to play a song called "You're the Top."

Now came the final part of Mrs. Honeybee's plan.

Once Wolf had become accustomed to showing up twice a day to get his chocolate from that spot above middle C, right in front of the lady's face, there came an evening when things were different. He arrived to find that there was no chocolate awaiting him. He looked down to see that the lady was holding the candy in the fingers of her left hand, while with her right she played, very softly, the melody of "Love's Old Sweet Song."

Mrs. Honeybee had worried about which song to choose at such an important moment. She had considered "Three Blind Mice" and "Come On, Everyone," but had decided that she would play the tune her mouse had been singing so sweetly when she had first opened the top of the piano and set eyes on him.

So now, in the twilight, she played this song in the high notes of the treble, gently waving the chocolate to and fro in time to the music. All the while she kept her eyes fixed on the mouse, willing him to do what she wanted. Sing for your supper, she thought, sing, sing, sing, like a good boy.

Wolf crouched stock-still, as quiet as a mouse indeed, listening to the melody and watching the little round piece of chocolate as it was waved in front of his nose.

Suddenly something clicked in his tiny brain. She wants me to sing for my supper, he said to himself, that's what she wants. I haven't got any words for this song, but perhaps it doesn't matter. He waited until the melody ended, then he sat up, straightened his whiskers with one paw, cleared his throat, and took a deep breath.

Right on cue Mrs. Honeybee once more began to play the tune with her right hand, and from the mouse's mouth there came again that high, pure, true voice.

"La-la-la-la-la-la!" caroled Wolf to Mrs. Honeybee's delighted accompaniment.

When the song ended, the accompanist gently held out her left hand to the singer, who took his reward, equally gently, in his two front paws.

- EIGHT -

A Groan

"DID MY EARS deceive me," said Mary when Wolf arrived home with his reward, "or were you singing at the same time as the lady was playing?"

"Yes, I was, Mommy," said Wolf. "It was fantastic!"

"How close to her were you?"

"Very close. I took this chocolate from her hand."

"You did *what?*" cried Mary. "You must be crazy!"

"Look, Mommy," said Wolf. "Tomorrow, when she comes to play

and I go up on the piano to sing, which I certainly intend to do, why don't you come with me?"

"I don't think so!" said Mary.

"What do you mean 'I don't think so!'?" said Wolf. "It seems to me that my mother is too scared. I'm not afraid, but you are."

Mary's eyes flashed.

"Wolfgang Amadeus!" she said. "Are you calling me a coward?"

"That remains to be seen," replied Wolf.

And seen it was, the following morning. To Mrs. Honeybee's surprise, not one but two mice appeared on the piano top. To be sure, the larger one seemed very wary, jumping nervously when the pianist raised her hands to play. But once the first bars of "Come On, Everyone" had rung out and the little mouse (could Mrs. Honeybee but have known it) was cheerfully singing "Merry mice are we! Mommy Mouse and me!" the other one (the mother, Mrs. Honeybee felt quite sure now) calmed down and sat listening proudly to her son.

Next the pianist played "Three Blind Mice" (and the singer sang "Singsong Mouse"). Mrs. Honeybee paused for Wolf to catch his breath.

The day's first chocolate, Wolf noted, was waiting there on the piano top, but he did not take it. Not only did he want to sing some more, but he also wanted to learn a new song (to impress his mother), and he stared beadily at Mrs. Honeybee, his eyes fixed on her, willing her to do what he wanted. Teach me a new song, he thought. Teach me, teach me, teach me, like a good woman.

Suddenly something clicked in Mrs. Honeybee's large brain. He wants to learn a new song, she thought, to impress his mother, I dare say. Perhaps his mother could learn it too, now that she's here. What a good idea! she decided. They can sing duets in close harmony. I'll try a cradle song, and then they'll be able to lull each other to sleep. She began to play, very quietly, the six-in-a-measure rhythm of a berceuse by Chopin.

After a while Wolf began to join in, and when she'd played the lullaby three times, he knew it by heart.

"Very nice, dear," said Mary when he had sung it right through. "I like that tune, though it does make me feel a bit sleepy."

"Why don't you give it a go, Mommy?" said Wolf, and at the same time Mrs. Honeybee, sitting and watching the two mice, heads close together, whiskers mingling, said, "Come on, mother mouse. You give it a shot."

"I can't sing," said Mary in answer to her son.

"How d'you know?" said Wolf. "You've never tried."

"Now, then, mother," said Mrs. Honeybee. "Here's your note."

"Go on, Mommy," said Wolf.

"Ready?" said Mrs. Honeybee. "One...two..." And Mary Mouse opened her mouth and out of it came a lot of hoarse, discordant squeaks.

"Oh, dear," said Mrs. Honeybee.

"Oh, dear," said Wolf.

"I told you!" said Mary angrily. "I suppose you think it's funny to make a fool of your old mother, Wolfgang Amadeus." And she flounced off.

Wolf followed, carrying the chocolate, while Mrs. Honeybee softly played and sang an old music-hall song that went:

> "Oh, dear, what can
> the matter be?"

That evening Wolf came alone.

The mother's taken umbrage, Mrs. Honeybee thought. Wherever my little mouse gets his voice from, it's certainly not from her. She played another new tune, a song by Schubert, and Wolf was very soon la-la-la-ing to it.

So quick and true was his musical ear that during the next few weeks he learned a good number of new songs. Not knowing any words to them didn't, he found, keep him from enjoying the sound of his own voice, and the more he learned, the more pleasure he got from his singing. The candy was very welcome, of course, but he would have sung away to the lady's accompaniment quite happily even if there had been no chocolate awaiting him.

And one morning there wasn't.

Wolf knew by now that very soon after the grandfather clock in the hall had struck eleven times, the lady would come into the living room to play. She would already have put a chocolate on the piano top, though Wolf never took it until after his singing was over.

That morning the clock struck, and after ten minutes or so, Wolf came out of the hole and ran up onto the piano top.

Funny, he thought, she's not usually late. He looked for the chocolate, but it wasn't there.

He waited. The house was very silent.

By the time the grandfather clock struck midday, Wolf was becoming worried. His relationship with his accompanist had become very close—sometimes, he felt, they could almost read each other's thoughts—and he now felt it was up to him to see if anything was the matter. I won't tell Mommy, he said to himself. She'll only forbid me to go.

The living room door was, as always, shut, but Wolf ran along a mouseway that came out into the hall and made his way toward the kitchen. As he entered it, he saw to his horror that the ginger cat was lying in its bed beside the stove. The cat's horror was, however, far greater. At the sight of the mouse it leaped up and disappeared through the cat flap at top speed.

Wolf looked around the kitchen

and then searched the other down-stairs rooms, but there was no sign of the lady.

Made bold by the flight of the cat, Wolf decided to go directly up the stairs. It was a long, steep climb, but he was young and fit, and he soon found himself on an upstairs landing, where he had never been before.

There were several doorways at the sides of this landing, and through one of them, an open one, Wolf sud-denly heard a groan.

NINE

A Rescue

MRS. HONEYBEE HAD awakened that morning expecting a perfectly ordinary day. As was now usual with her, she thought first of her mouse.

"My mice, I should say, I suppose, but of course the mother is just an average mouse," she said. "Whereas my little mouse is the eighth wonder of the world! How beautifully he sings, and how well we communicate now—I teach, he learns, and so quickly, too. What a pity it is that humans and animals can't communicate directly by speech. I could say 'I'm Jane Honeybee,' and he would reply 'And I'm Whatever-it-is'—I really ought to give him a name—and I'd say 'What kind of song would you like me to teach you today?' and he might say 'Oh, something cheery because it's a lovely day,' and then I might play 'Oh, What a Beautiful Mornin'!' from the musical *Oklahoma!*"

Mrs. Honeybee got out of bed and washed and dressed, went downstairs, made herself some breakfast, and fed the cat.

Later that morning, after she had puttered around the garden for a while and was thinking about going to the living room to put out a chocolate for the morning playing, she suddenly remembered that she'd forgotten to make her bed.

She went upstairs and stood at the open bedroom window for a moment, looking down the sunlit street and whistling "Oh, What a Beautiful Mornin'!" But then suddenly it wasn't.

As Mrs. Honeybee turned away from the window, momentarily blinded by the glare of the sunlight, she tripped over a small footstool and fell. Because she was old and stiff, she fell awkwardly, and as she hit the ground she heard a horrible cracking sound and felt a white-hot pain in one ankle.

For a while she lay in a state of shock, but then she began to try to get to her feet (or rather to one foot—the other, she realized, could not possibly have any weight put on it). But she was quite shaky and her efforts were in vain.

"Oh, dear, Jane Honeybee!" she gasped as she lay on her bedroom floor. "What in the world's to become of you?" And, half-fainting because the pain was so sharp, she gave a groan.

Wolf, running into the bedroom at the sound, was mystified. Why was the lady lying on the floor with her eyes closed? And that groan had been a most unhappy noise.

I must try to brighten her up, he thought, and in the most cheerful voice he could manage, he began to sing his version of the words to:

"Come on, everyone!
    Sing and dance and run!
    Making friends and
    Having a lot of fun!"

Mrs. Honeybee opened her eyes.

"Oh, mouse!" she said. "You certainly are a good pal. You must have been wondering where I'd gone. You haven't had your morning chocolate, and I was going to teach you a new song, too. Oh, dear, oh, dear! If only you could understand me, I'd ask you to go downstairs and pick up the phone and dial 911, and when they ask 'What is wrong?' you could answer 'Mrs. Honeybee needs an ambulance.' I need help, mouse, I need help."

Wolf of course could not understand a word of this, but some instinct told him that the lady was in trouble. I can't do anything, he thought. She needs a human being to come to her aid. And where are there other humans? Out on the street!

He ran across the room and climbed up the curtains and onto the windowsill. Mrs. Honeybee's house was on a quiet tree-lined street where many people were not usually about. But at that very moment a man appeared, walking at a leisurely pace along the sidewalk toward the house. He was a tallish man, Wolf saw as he peered down, and he was dressed in a dark blue uniform and wearing a cap. His boots were big and black.

No good squeaking at him, Wolf thought. I must sing as loud as I can to attract his attention. What shall I sing? Quickly he thought about some new songs that he had learned. Mrs. Honeybee's taste in music was broad, and by chance she had recently taught Wolf an old Beatles song.

At the top of his voice Wolf began to sing "Help!"

At the sound of that voice, so high, so pure, so true, the policeman stopped on his patrol and looked up at the bedroom window. Not only was he the local community police-man, but he also sang in the police choir, and what's more, he was friendly with old Mrs. Honeybee, knowing her onetime reputation as a concert pianist. Sometimes, as he walked along the street, he had heard her singing as she played. But this was not her voice. This was in a far

higher register. In fact, it was the voice of a coloratura soprano.

The policeman squinted upward, but he could see nothing, for Wolf was hidden from his gaze by the ivy that covered the house. He stood a moment, smiling, for the voice, whoever it belonged to, was a very lovely one. Must be a recording she's playing, he thought as the song ended.

He was about to walk on when he thought he heard a noise coming from the bedroom, a noise that sounded almost like a groan.

"I hope the old lady's all right," he said to himself, and he went and knocked on the front door, then rang the bell.

No one came.

He looked through the letter slot and saw letters scattered on the hall floor. "Mrs. Honeybee!" the policeman shouted up at the bedroom window. "Is everything all right?" And in reply he heard a feeble "No."

Quickly the policeman used his radio to contact his station sergeant. "It's Mrs. Honeybee," he said. "You know, the pianist lady. She's in trouble, I think, Sarge. Better send for an ambulance. I'll try to get into the house."

So it was that Wolf's singing brought help. The policeman borrowed a ladder from a neighbor and climbed up and through the open bedroom window to comfort Mrs. Honeybee and then to let the paramedics in when they arrived.

Wolf, hiding behind the curtains, watched as, very carefully, the paramedics lifted the lady onto a stretcher.

"The cat!" she said as they loaded her into the ambulance. "Who will feed the cat?"

"Don't worry, Mrs. H.," said the policeman. "I'll go right now and ask the next-door neighbors to do it." And off he went.

"But what about my mice?" said

Mrs. Honeybee. "Who'll give them their chocolate candy?"

"She's wandering in her mind a bit," said one of the paramedics.

"It's the pain," said his partner.

"Your mice will be all right," they said.

"To think," said Mrs. Honeybee, "that I was going to teach him 'Oh, What a Beautiful Mornin'!'"

"Teach who?" said the first paramedic.

"My little mouse. He sings beautifully, you know."

"Yes, love," said the second soothingly. "Of course he does."

- TEN -

A Composer

IF MRS. HONEYBEE had been young, the hospital would have set her broken ankle, put it in a cast or a bandage, and sent her home in no time at all.

As it was, the doctors decided to keep her in for a while because of the shock she had suffered, and because she did not quite seem to be in her right mind. She kept worrying, the nurses said, about a singing mouse to whom she was teaching songs!

So Wolf and Mary were alone in

the house (apart from the cat, which they now never saw, and those brothers and sisters of Wolf who had not moved out but who never came back to the living room anyway).

Mary did not particularly miss the lady, but she did miss the chocolates. She had become hooked on them and was now suffering severe withdrawal symptoms. These made her short-tempered, and a good deal of the time she addressed her son as Wolfgang Amadeus.

Wolf missed his friend badly. What's more, he had no idea when she would return. How he longed to see her sitting at the piano, smiling at him (for he now knew that when she showed her teeth at him, it did not— as would have been the case with most animals—mean that she was angry with him, but rather the reverse).

He missed his singing lessons very much, and though he practiced his scales every day as she had taught him, and sang all the songs he'd learned, it wasn't the same without the accompanist.

Nor, of course, was he hearing any new melodies.

One evening when Mrs. Honeybee had been in the hospital for four or five days, Wolf was sitting and thinking on the piano stool—it made him feel closer to his friend—when suddenly an idea occurred to him.

She's not here to teach me new tunes, but why don't I make up my own music? Has any mouse ever composed music before, I wonder? No. But then has any mouse ever sung the way I can? Why shouldn't I be a composer as well as a singer? Think how surprised she'll be when I sing my own music to her, my very own, and I don't mean dumpty-dumpty-dumpty stuff, but really difficult music like she sometimes plays, where I can really use my voice to the best advantage. What's more, if I sing this piece of music—whatever it turns out to be—often enough to her, she can learn to play it, and then she can accompany me.

What a pity it is that animals and humans can't communicate directly by speech. She could say "I'm Whoever-it-is"—I really ought to give her a name—and I'd say "I am the composer Wolfgang Amadeus Mouse."

Composition, Wolf found, was not at all easy. He spent many hours sitting on the piano top, warbling away without producing anything that satisfied him (he didn't bother with words; the melodies were what interested him).

Then one day he hit upon a theme that he immediately knew would be the backbone of his piece.

He was sitting, not on the piano but upstairs on the sill of the now-closed window in the lady's bedroom. He looked out, and there, high up in the sky, were swallows, hawking for insects in the warm evening air. A swooping, twisting, darting melody came into his head ready-made.

As he sang the first few bars of it, Wolf felt suddenly inspired, and the music poured out of his mouth as his voice swooped and twisted and darted like the birds. Somehow he seemed to know instinctively where this musical work of his would start, and the way it would continue, and how it would end. And when it did end, he sang it again and again, until he had every note firmly fixed in his head.

Then he ran downstairs to find his mother.

"Mommy!" he cried. "What d'you think! I am a composer!"

"Composer?" said Mary Mouse crustily (for she was missing those chocolate candies). "What on earth does that mean, Wolfgang Amadeus?"

"I have made up some music of my very own," said Wolf. "Shall I sing it to you?"

"If you must," said Mary.

Truth to tell, she had a very poor musical ear, and though she was proud of her son's talents, she derived little pleasure from most of the songs he sang. But now as she listened, she found herself at first interested, and then moved, and finally captivated by the beauty of the music that he was singing, by its lightness, its airiness, its sheer joyfulness.

"Oh, Wolf dear!" she said when he had finished. "That was really lovely! Does it have a name?"

"Yes," said Wolf. "That is my 'Swallow Sonata.'"

- ELEVEN -

A Recital

WHEN MRS. HONEYBEE did come home, she was on crutches and a nurse was with her. The first thing Mrs. Honeybee thought about was her mouse, but she didn't say anything to the nurse. She had realized that in the hospital she had babbled on a bit about her singing mouse—they had probably thought she was senile— but now that she was back home, she knew that she wanted the matter kept secret. If it got out that she had the world's first singing mouse beneath her roof, the publicity would be overwhelming and she would never again have a moment's peace.

The first thing she did was to go to her grand piano and, leaning one crutch against the wall and balancing with the other, tap out with one finger "There's No Place Like Home."

"You'll have a tough time playing, dear," said the nurse, "with that foot in a cast."

"I'll just have to manage with one pedal for the time being," said Mrs. Honeybee.

"Well, I'll tell you one thing you won't be able to manage," said the nurse, "and that's the stairs. We'll have to make you up a bed downstairs. Where shall it be? In your den?"

"No, here, please," said Mrs.

Honeybee. "Here in the living room, right next to my beloved piano."

And very near my beloved mouse, she thought.

"There's a sort of daybed," she said, "that I use out in the garden. You'll find it in the conservatory at the back of the house. I'll be with you in half a minute." And when the nurse had left the room, she hopped across to the candy tin. She opened a fresh packet of chocolates, then put not one but two on the piano stool before following the nurse.

When they came back to make up the bed, the chocolates, Mrs. Honeybee saw immediately, were gone.

"Look, Mommy!" Wolf had said. "One each!"

"Thank goodness!" Mary had

cried, and she had begun to gobble her chocolate like a crazy thing.

Once she was sure that Mrs. Honeybee had everything she wanted, the nurse left, saying that she would be back the next morning. As soon as she had gone, Mrs. Honeybee put out another double ration of candy, on the piano top this time, and sat on the stool and waited.

In the mousehole Mary said, "She's put out some more, I can smell it. Come on, Wolf!"

"Okay, Mommy," said Wolf, and together they came out and ran up the leg of the piano and onto the top.

"One each again!" squeaked Mary, and she attacked her chocolate eagerly.

Wolf did not touch his. Instead he

sat above middle C, above STEINWAY & SONS, and gazed fondly at Mrs. Honeybee's face while she gazed fondly back.

Oh, how glad I am to see you again, each thought. (Mary thought the same, but she was referring to the chocolate candy.)

Should I sing to her? wondered Wolf. Should I sing her my very own composition now?

But then something told him, No, this is not the moment. I want her to hear it first when we're alone together. Mommy might interrupt, and anyway she's making a lot of noise gobbling chocolate. I'll wait for the right time.

"Tomorrow," said Mrs. Honeybee, "we'll have some music, okay, mouse? Just now I'm going to bed. I'm a bit tired."

However, that night she could not get to sleep. It was so odd to be in bed in the living room, beside the grand piano. But then, maybe by chance, or maybe because he sensed that this was what a cradle song was designed to do, Wolf began to sing, very softly, the Chopin lullaby. In a matter of minutes, Mrs. Honeybee fell asleep.

In the days that followed, Wolf, sometimes accompanied, sometimes not, sang all the songs that he'd learned, including a new one (for the weather was still fine and Mrs. Honeybee had at last taught him "Oh, What a Beautiful Mornin'!").

But very often at night, when she

was fast asleep in the living room, Wolf ran upstairs to practice and perfect his own composition in her bedroom.

Meanwhile, Mrs. Honeybee progressed from crutches to canes, and from two canes to one, and then she went back to the hospital to have the cast removed and to be told that her ankle had healed beautifully. She came home, walking without a cane at all, and that night she climbed the stairs to sleep in her own room.

She had said good night to the mice and had given them one chocolate each. She didn't have the heart to go back to the old ration of one between the two of them. Mary didn't mind. She ate hers and what Wolf couldn't manage.

Mrs. Honeybee lay in bed, remembering her fall and how painful it had been and how the nice policeman had come climbing through the window. It was open now, the curtains drawn back so that the streetlight outside filled the room with a soft glow.

"How did the man know I was in trouble?" she said. "I can't really recall what happened, but I thought my mouse was there, singing. No, no, I must have imagined all that."

And then she heard a little rustling noise, which was Wolf scrambling up the curtains, and there he was, her singing mouse, sitting on the windowsill facing her. He stood up on his hind legs for a moment and dropped his head slightly, almost as though he were bowing to her, she thought. Then he began to sing his "Swallow Sonata."

Mrs. Honeybee lay spellbound. I never taught him this, she thought, I've never heard this piece of music before. Never in all my concert-playing days did I hear this, and yet it must be by one of the great classical composers. How light it is, how airy, how sheerly joyful!

But how can my mouse know it? All he has learned he has learned from me. There can be only one explanation. *He* has composed it. It is his very own opus!

Then with a final reprise of its principal swooping, twisting, darting bird theme, the song ended, and Wolf sat silent on the sill.

"Oh, mouse!" cried Mrs. Honeybee, clapping her hands. "What a piece of work is this! You must teach it to me, mouse. Tomorrow you must sing it through to me again and again, and I will somehow force my rheumaticky old fingers to play all those lovely lilting notes. Why, Mozart could not have composed anything more entrancing, mouse. Which gives me a sudden idea, a brilliant idea if I say so myself, for a name to call you, instead of always saying 'mouse.' Mozart, you see, was not only the greatest of musicians, he was also the most precocious. He began to compose at a very early age, just like you. So why don't I call you by his name?"

Wolf listened to the lady, without

of course understanding a word that she said. She was pleased, though, he felt sure. She approved of his "Swallow Sonata," and he felt glad and proud.

He saw her get out of bed and approach the window and stretch out an arm toward him very slowly.

Then with one finger Mrs. Honeybee very gently stroked him on top of his sleek brown head.

"Mozart's name," she said, "was Wolfgang Amadeus, so that is what I am going to call you from now on. No, wait a bit, that's too much of a mouthful, I think. Why don't I just call you Wolf?"

She smiled happily to herself.

"You really are a ridiculous old woman, Jane Honeybee," she said.

THOMAS FORD MEMORIAL LIBRARY
WESTERN SPRINGS, IL 60558

"Who but you would think of something so unlikely as a mouse called Wolf!"

ABOUT THE AUTHOR

DICK KING-SMITH was born and raised in Gloucestershire, England. He served in the Grenadier Guards during World War II, then returned home to Gloucestershire to realize his lifelong ambition of farming. After twenty years as a farmer, he turned to teaching and then to writing the children's books that have earned him many fans on both sides of the Atlantic. Inspiration for his writing has come from his farm and his animals.

Among his well-loved novels are *Babe: The Gallant Pig*, *Harry's Mad*, *Ace: The Very Important Pig*, *Three Terrible Trins*, *Harriet's Hare*, and *The Stray*. In 1992 he was named Children's Author of the Year at the British Book Awards. In 1995 *Babe: The Gallant Pig* became a critically acclaimed major motion picture.